The Old Woman Who Lived in a Vinegar Bottle

A BRITISH FAIRY TALE

Margaret Read MacDonald

Illustrations by
Nancy Dunaway Fowlkes

AUGUST HOUSE
Littlefolk

For Jane of the Happy House
— M.R.M.

For Eula, David, Caroline & Annie
— N.D.F.

Text © 1995 by Margaret Read MacDonald
Illustrations © 1995 by Nancy Dunaway Fowlkes

Published 1995 by August House LittleFolk,
P.O. Box 3223, Little Rock, Arkansas 72203,
501-372-5450.

Book design by Harvill Ross Studios Ltd., Little Rock

Manufactured in Hong Kong

10 9 8 7 6 5 4 3 2 1

LIBRARY OF CONGRESS CATALOGING-IN-PUBLICATION DATA

MacDonald, Margaret Read, 1940–
The old woman who lived in a vinegar bottle / Margaret Read MacDonald;
illustrations by Nancy Dunaway Fowlkes.
        p.   cm.
Summary: In this British variant of a traditional tale, an ungrateful woman
who complains constantly about her house is granted increasingly grandiose
wishes by a fairy.
ISBN 0-87483-415-5: $15.95
[l. Fairy tales. 2. Folklore—Great Britain.]
I. Fowlkes, Nancy Dunaway, 1947–   , ill.   II. Title.
PZ8.M175501   1995
398.2´0941´01—dc20
[E]   94-46967

The paper used in this publication meets the minimum requirements of the
American National Standards for Information Sciences—
permanence of Paper for Printed Library Materials, ANSI.48-1984

ABOUT THE STORY

Katharine Briggs heard this as a campfire story in 1924 and printed it in *A Dictionary of British Folk-Tales* (Bloomington: Indiana University Press, 1970). Another delightful version is the picture book by Rumer Godden (New York: Viking Press, 1970), who heard the story told in her family. My version has been honed through hundreds of tellings in my work as a librarian and storyteller.

Though only a few variants of our "vinegar bottle " story have been collected, a similar tale, "The Fisherman and His Wife," is widely known. In the Brothers Grimm version a magic fish grants wishes for a fisherman's wife. Our British story replaces the magic fish with a fairy, and while the Grimms place the fisherman's wife in a shack, our version goes one step further and puts the poor woman in a vinegar bottle!

The Aarne-Thompson Type Index lists variants from more than 30 countries under Type 555, *The Fisher and His Wife.* For more variants in children's books see motif B375.1 *Fish returned to water: grateful* in *The Storyteller's Sourcebook* by Margaret Read MacDonald (Detroit: Gale Research, 1982).

This is a wonderful story for making the leap from readaloud to active storytelling. It is easy to remember, and whether you are reading at home or in a classroom, children love to chime in on the repeated phrases. The old woman should be whiny, of course; and you can have fun giving the fairy an attitude, too.

— *M.R.M.*

There once was an old woman who lived in a *vinegar bottle*.
Don't ask me why. It was a common old vinegar bottle.
Unusually large, of course.
Still, it did make a very small house.

Every day the old woman would sit on her step and complain.
"Oh, what a pity!
What a pity pity pity!
That I should have to live in a tiny little house such as this.
Why, *I* should be living in a cottage
with a thatched roof and roses growing up the walls.
That's what *I* deserve."

Just then a fairy happened to be passing by.

"I could do *that*," thought the fairy.

"If that's what she wants . . .

that's what she'll *get*."

And to the old woman she said,

"When you go to bed tonight,

turn around three times and close your eyes.

In the morning, see what you shall see."

The old woman thought the fairy was likely batty.

But when she went to bed that night,

she turned around three times and closed her eyes.

In the morning, when she opened them again . . .

She was in a dear little cottage!
With a thatched roof
and roses growing up the walls!
    "It's just what I've always wanted,"
    she said."How content I'll be living *here*."
But she said not a word of thanks to
the fairy.

Well, the fairy went north
and the fairy went south.
The fairy went east
and the fairy went west.
She did all the business she had to do.

Then she started thinking ...

"I wonder how that old woman is doing,
the one who used to live in a vinegar bottle."

But when the fairy came near,
there sat the old woman . . . *complaining*.

"Oh what a pity!

What a pity pity pity!

That I should have to live in a tiny little cottage
like this. Why, I should be living in a fine row house
with lace curtains at the windows and a brass
knocker on the door!"

"I can do *that*," thought the fairy.

"If that's what she wants . . .

that's what she'll *get*."

And to the old woman she said,

"When you go to bed tonight,

turn around three times and close your eyes.

In the morning, see what you shall see."

The old woman didn't have to be told twice.

She went right to bed.

She turned around three times and closed her eyes.

In the morning when she opened them . . .

She was in a spanking new row house!
With lace curtains at the windows and a brass
knocker on the door.

"It's just what I always wanted," said the old
woman. "I'll be so contented *here*."
But she never said a word of thanks to the fairy.

Well, the fairy went north
and the fairy went south.
The fairy went east
and the fairy went west.
She did all the business she had to do.

Then she thought about that old woman.
"I wonder how that old woman is doing
these days . . . the one that used to live in the
vinegar bottle."

But when the fairy came to the fine row house,

there sat the old woman in her brand new rocking chair . . .

complaining.

    "Oh, what a pity!

    What a pity pity pity!

    That I should have to live in a row house like this,

    with common folk on either side.

    I should live in a mansion on the hill

    with servants to do my bidding.

    That's what *I* deserve."

When the fairy heard that, she was much amazed.

But she said,

    "Well, if that's what she wants . . .

    That's what she'll *get*."

And to the old woman she said,

    "When you go to bed tonight,

    turn around three times and close your eyes.

    In the morning, see what you shall see."

The old woman turned around three times and hopped into bed. She

closed her eyes, and in the morning, when she opened them again . . .

She was in a mansion on the hill!

"This is just what I've always wanted," said the old woman.

"How contented I will be *here*."

But it never occurred to her to thank the fairy.

Well, the fairy went north

and the fairy went south.

The fairy went east

and the fairy went west.

She did all the business she had to do.

Then she remembered the old woman again.

"I wonder how that old woman is getting on now . . .

the old woman who used to live in a vinegar bottle."

But when she came near, there sat the old woman in her velvet chair . . . *complaining*.

> "Oh, what a pity!
> What a pity pity pity!
> That I should have to live in an old mansion like this.
> Why, I should be the *queen* living in the *palace,* with musicians to entertain me and courtiers to bow to me.
> That's what I deserve."

"Good heavens," thought the fairy.
"Will she *never* be content?

> Well, if that's what she wants . . .
> that's what she'll *get*."

To the old woman she said,

"When you go to bed tonight,

turn around three times and close your eyes.

In the morning, see what you shall see."

The old woman hurried to bed.

She turned around three times.

She closed her eyes.

In the morning . . .

She was in the *palace!*

With musicians to entertain her and courtiers to bow and bow.

"This is just what I've always wanted," said the old woman.

"I will be very contented now."

But she forgot entirely to thank the fairy.

Well, the fairy went north
and the fairy went south.
The fairy went east
and the fairy went west.
She did all the business she had to do.

Then she began to think: "I wonder how that old woman is getting along . . . the one who used to live in a vinegar bottle."

But when she got to the palace,
there sat the old woman on her throne . . .
complaining!

"Oh, what a pity!
What a pity pity pity!
That I should be queen of such a tiny kingdom.
Why, I should be the Empress of the Universe.
Empress of the Universe!
That's what I deserve."

"I see!" said the fairy. "There's
no pleasing some people.

If that's what she wants . . .
that's what she'll *not* get!"

And to the old woman she said,

"When you go to bed tonight,

turn around three times and close your eyes.

In the morning, *see what you shall see.*"

The old woman went right to bed.

She turned around three times.

She closed her eyes.

And in the morning, when she opened them . . .

She was right back in her vinegar bottle!
"And there she shall stay," said the fairy.
    "If she's not content here,
    she won't be content *there*."

After all,
happiness comes from the heart,
not from the house.